Series 401

A Ladybird Book

BUNNY'S FIRST BIRTHDAY tells all about Baby Bunny's invitation to his little farmyard friends, and how amazed and enchanted they were when they came to his party. The verses delightfully describe the many good things they enjoyed.

BUNNY'S FIRST BIRTHDAY

Story and illustrations by A. J. MACGREGOR

Verses by W. PERRING

Ladybird Books Loughborough

Baby Bunny, on his birthday,
　　Sat on Mummy Bunny's knee,
While she wrote a little letter
　　Asking all his friends to tea.

Off they pattered to the farmyard,
　　Knocked and knocked upon the door;
Farmyard folk were busy eating,
　　Didn't know the feast in store!

Baby handed in the letter;

Farmyard folk, in great surprise,

Squawked and squeaked and squealed
and grunted
All at once, and blinked their eyes.

Mother Goose read out the letter

    To the babies round the yard;

But with all the squeaks and chatter,

    Hearing it was rather hard.

To The
Babies

What a bathing and a brushing
　　And a combing now began!
Mother Hutch's twins were naughty,
　　For at first, they squealed and ran!

Then, with sponge and soap and water,
　　Fluff and Brownie in the hutch,
Had a lovely wash, that made them
　　Clean and smooth and soft to touch.

In their wooden tub, the Quackies

    Seemed to think it rather fun!

Mother Quack had little trouble,

    Quackies' bathing soon was done!

Piggly-Wriggly started squealing

    When the soap got in his eye;

Squiggly swallowed soapy water,

    Spluttered and began to cry!

Mother Hen upon the cobbles

    Placed her chickens in a row,

Felt so proud about their cleanness

    That she nearly tried to crow!

"Look!" said Mr. Mouse, "The barrow

In the corner by the wall

Makes a lovely carriage. Try it!"

But it wouldn't move at all.

Mr. Burly Pig just grunted,

   Came across and wheeled it round—

Pushing it about the farmyard,

   Rumble-bump along the ground.

Now the crowd of farmyard babies

    Came and packed themselves inside;

Pigglies, Mousies, Quackies, Bunnies,

    Chicks—and Lambkin—for the ride.

Mr. Pig was very careful

    Going through the farmyard gate.

"Hurry!" cried the babies, "Hurry!

    Do you want us to be late?"

All the farmyard folk, excited,

    Came and waved them all goodbye.

Off they started down the hill-side

    Quacking, squeaking, bleating " Hi ! "

By her window Mrs. Bunny

Waited, but the path was steep,

And the barrow started slipping

And the stream was wet and deep!

Quick as lightning, Father Bunny

    Put a log beneath the wheel;

Over went the loaded barrow!

    Piggly gave a frightened squeal!

Down they shot into the water,

　　Mice and Quackies all could swim.

Piggly only splashed and spluttered!

　　How the fishes laughed at him!

As the other babes were landing,

    Piggly kicked and rolled about;

While he struggled, Father Bunny

    Fetched a rope and helped him out.

So, once more, to Bunny's party
    Off they went. And little Mouse
Ran in front and knocked. The babies
    Soon arrived at Bunny House.

Mr. Bunny cuddled Piggly
    To his fur, so warm and soft,
Lest he should be feeling chilly—
    Piggly never even coughed!

When the babies saw the banquet

And the cake, they were amazed;

Stood enchanted in the doorway

Open mouthed, and gazed and gazed.

Piggly's cheeks were full of acorns!

Mousies nibbled tasty cheese!

Never was a birthday party

With such dainty foods as these!

Bunnies at their lettuce salad

    Crunched and munched with shining
                              eyes;
Golden buttercups for Lambkin

    Made her stare in glad surprise.

Quackies pulled and tugged and swallowed

Lovely worms with all their might;

Chicks were pecking in their basins

Yellow corn, in great delight.

And as Bunny cut the slices,

    Little mouse could scarcely wait.

How they loved the fruit and icing,

    Every baby cleared his plate.

Then the birthday party ended—

    Piggly's skin was very tight;

Up came Mr. Pig to fetch them,

    So the babies said "Goodnight."

Mr. Pig was heavy-laden,

Homeward bound beneath the moon,

Past the owl upon the sign post . . .

Babies would be sleeping soon.

The first light bulbs
did not last for long.
Today, light bulbs
last for a very
long time.

Before credit cards were invented, people had to pay for everything with paper money or coins.

The first telephones were connected by wires. Today, mobile phones can be used anywhere.

Before motor cars were invented, people had to walk or ride horses to get from one place to another.

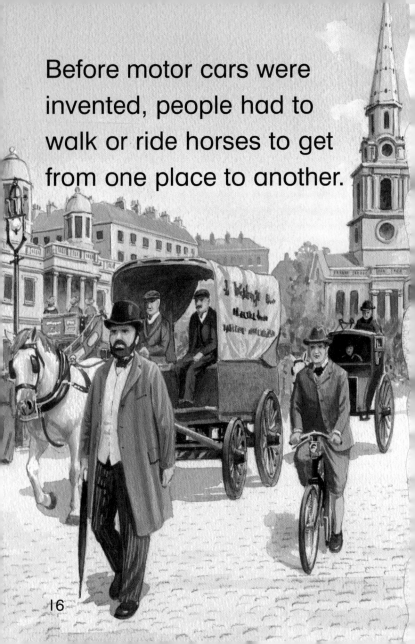

The first motor cars were very slow.
Today, cars are very fast.

Before zips were invented, people had to fasten their clothes with lots of buttons and hooks.

It used to take a long time to get dressed. Today, clothes are easy to put on and take off using zips.

Before televisions were invented, people could not see what was happening in other countries.

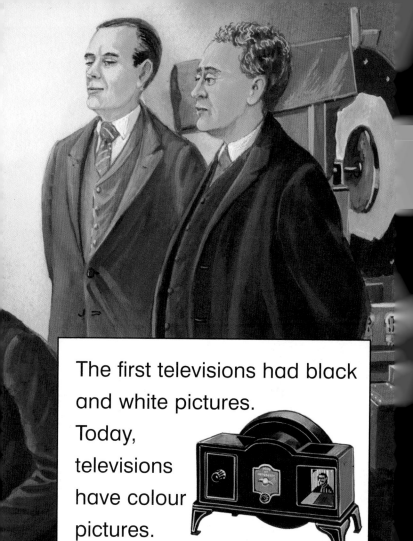

The first televisions had black and white pictures. Today, televisions have colour pictures.

Before dishwashers were invented, people had to wash and dry plates, glasses and cutlery by hand.

The first dishwashers were only used in restaurants. Today, dishwashers are used in homes, too.

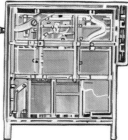

Before light bulbs were invented, people used candles, oil lamps or gas lamps to see at night.